Fierce Milly

Stornoway Primary School
Jamieson Drive
STORNOWAY
Isle of Lewis HS1 2LF
TEL: (01851) 703418 / 703621

If you enjoy reading this book, you might
also like to try another story
from the **MAMMOTH STORYBOOK** series:

Fierce Milly

Marilyn McLaughlin

illustrated by Leonie Shearing

mammoth

To Secnarf and Nhoj
M.M.

To Jerry and Cheryl
thanks for everything
L.S.

First published in Great Britain in 1999
by Mammoth, an imprint of Egmont Children's Books Limited
239 Kensington High Street, London, W8 6SA

Text copyright © 1999 Marilyn McLaughlin
Illustrations copyright © 1999 Leonie Shearing

The moral rights of the author and illustrator have been asserted

The rights of Marilyn McLaughlin and Leonie Shearing to be
identified as the author and illustrator of this work have been asserted by
them in accordance with the Copyright, Designs and Patents Act 1988

ISBN 0 7497 3731 X

10 9 8 7 6 5 4 3 2 1

A CIP catalogue record for this book
is available from the British Library

Printed in Great Britain by Cox & Wyman Ltd,
Reading, Berkshire

Contents

~

1 Fierce Milly and the yellow hand

Our Billy was mixing boring paints. He made purple and orange and green. Then he mixed them all together and made yucky brown. Then he said that he had made chocolate.

'It's not chocolate, it's only boring old paint,' I said.

'Now that's enough, Susan,' Mum said. 'Go out and play with your friend Joe if everything's boring.'

'There's no one to play with. Joe is in a

boring old gang with Cecil Nutt today and they won't let me be in it because I'm a girl.'

'I know what you can do,' said Mum. 'There's new people moved into the street, and they have a little girl just your age. Go and call for her, and take Billy with you. He's too little to play on his own.'

'What's her name?' I said.

'Mildred, I think,' said Mum. 'She'll be very nice because I used to go to school with her mother and she was lovely.'

Mum was wrong about that. Going to school with somebody's mother does not make them nice. Me and Billy went round to the new people's house and rang the doorbell. The next best thing to a monster jumped out at us. It had a spear and a big shield and it had been eating an ice pop that made its mouth all bright red. It was sticking its tongue out and hopping all round us, roaring every so often.

'Are you
Mildred?'
asked
our Billy.

'Never call me
Mildred or your
tongue will fall out
and land on the
ground at your feet
and just lie there looking at you. I am Milly,
Fierce Milly. Fierce Milly for ever.' And she
did a little war dance round the garden.

'Where did you get the spear?' Billy
asked.

'From my uncle that came
back from Africa,' she said.
'He is fierce as a lion, fierce
as a buffalo, fierce as a
volcano, but he's not as fierce as
me.' And she roared again.

'Great roar,' said Billy. 'Does it hurt

3

your throat?'

'Nothing hurts Fierce Milly. And who are you anyway, squirt?'

'I'm Billy,' said Billy. 'And that's my big sister, Susan.'

'Well get out of my garden you both, this is my jungle and there's only me allowed in it.'

So we got out.

'I don't want to play with her anyway,' said Billy.

'Neither do I,' I said. 'Let's go home.'

We went home the back way because it's the longest, and we didn't want to go home just yet. There was a surprise. The new people had painted their backyard door yellow.

It was very yellow, very, very yellow. Billy started one of his chants. 'It's so yellow it tastes of melty butter. It's so yellow it sizzles like eggs frying. It's so yellow it stings hard as wasps. It's so yellow ...'

'Shut up, Billy,' I said. 'Doors can't sting.'

'It's so yellow it smells like bananas.'

'Shut up, Billy.'

The next day Billy wanted to see the yellow door again, but there was a big surprise when we got there. Written right across the middle of the yellow door, in big black

letters, was:

'Mill-dread rules. Go in fear!'

And there was also a not-very-good drawing of a skull and crossbones.

'Is that her name?' asked Billy. 'Is that how you spell Mildred?'

'No, she's just trying to be frightening.'

'To fill our hearts with nameless dread,' said Billy, who sometimes says very queer things.

'She'll be filled with nameless dread when her mum sees that,' I said.

The next day our mum said, 'That nice Milly is putting another coat of paint on their backyard door. What a lovely helpful child.'

So me and Billy ran out to the back lane to watch the lovely helpful child, from a safe distance.

Fierce Milly was painting over her name with yellow paint, but before she got it finished she put a yellow hand on everything. She put one on Mr McMichael's bin and one on the tin door down the lane. She even put an invisible yellow hand on the yellow door.

Then she saw us and tried to put a yellow hand on Billy, but he was too fast for her. He scooted off and she ran after him shouting, 'I'm the yellow-hand monster.'

And then her mum came flying out of their backyard and shouted, 'Mildred!' That

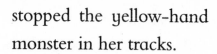

stopped the yellow-hand monster in her tracks.

Fierce Milly's mum was cross about all the yellow hands in the back lane and she made Fierce Milly scrub them off. Me and Billy stayed to watch in case she did anything else interesting. She might be fierce, but she was not boring.

'All gone,' Fierce Milly said when she had finished. 'Except for the invisible one on the yellow door. Nobody else knows it's there. We're a secret society now.'

'What's a secret society?' asked Billy.

'It's like Joe's and Cecil Nutt's gang, when you don't let anyone else play with you,' I said.

'Would it be good?' asked Billy.

'Might be,' I said.

'I'm the boss of the gang and you're my slaves and you have to do what I tell you,' said Fierce Milly.

This was not good. 'What makes you the boss?' I asked.

'Because it's my hand on the door and, if you don't do what I say, the secret yellow hand will come off the yellow door, and it will come after you, and it will pinch all your sweets, and it will draw on your books, and it will change the channel on the TV, and it will pull the plug out when you're in the bath …it will …'

You could see she was thinking up something really terrible.

'It will flush the toilet when you're

9

still sitting on it! And all sorts of other things too, only I haven't thought of them yet.'

'Let it,' I said. 'See if I care.'

'In, Mildred!' Fierce Milly's mum came back. 'You're not out of trouble yet.' And Fierce Milly had to go in the back door. But she stuck out one hand behind her and waved it at us. It was still yellow. Our Billy had gone all pale, the way he does just before he's sick. 'Can that yellow hand really do all that?' he asked.

'Course not. It's only paint, silly. None of those things can happen for real, she's just making them up to scare you because she wants to be boss of our gang.'

'I'm scared,' said Billy. 'I'm not ever going

to the toilet ever again. I'm not ever going to have a bath ever again.'

Billy thinks that if you pull the plug before you get out of the bath, you might go down the plughole. He looked really sad and very scared. I was sorry for him, so I had a think.

'I know how to fix that old hand,' I said. 'Come with me.'

I got a pot of paint out of our garage. It was left over when Billy's bedroom was painted. It was blue.

'Blue as the sky, blue as the sea, blue as a monkey's bottom . . .' said Billy.

'Shut up, Billy, we have to be quick.'

So me and Billy scooted up the back lane to the yellow door.

'I'm scared,' said Billy.

'You're all right,' I said. 'I'm with you. Where's the yellow hand?'

'Right there in the middle, I remember,' said Billy.

'Certain sure?'

'Certain sure. I can see it! I can see it!'

I slapped a great big blue hand right on top of where Billy said he could see the yellow one.

'There! Now it can't get off the door. It's stuck under my blue hand.'

'Oooooooh!' said Billy, all smiles. 'So it is!'

'Hey! What are you doing to my door?' came a big shout from nowhere. Billy jumped the height of himself and looked up the lane and down the lane.

'It's Fierce Milly,' he said. 'She's invisible!'

'I'm up here,' she roared.

She was right up on top of

her backyard wall.

'How did you get up there?' Billy asked.

'I jumped up,' she said. 'I've got special spring-sprung knees. I can jump over houses. I can jump over trees.'

'Well jump on down here, then, and see what has happened your door,' I shouted.

Fierce Milly climbed down the wall, very carefully for someone who had spring-sprung knees, and looked at the blue hand on the yellow hand on the yellow door.

'What's that, then?' she roared and her face squeezed up into a big frown.

'It's my blue hand and it's on top of your yellow one,' I said. 'So it's the blue hand gang and I'm boss of it.'

Fierce Milly thought for a moment. Then she said, 'Let's not bother with bosses. Let's just all be friends.'

'All right,' I said.

'But I'm still fiercer than you,' she said.

'All right,' Billy said.

'And I'm going to get some more yellow paint to cover that up before my mum sees it,' Fierce Milly said.

While she was gone, Billy asked, 'Can she really jump over trees?'

'Oh, Billy, will you stop believing things. She just made that up . . . I think.'

2 Fierce Milly in the Old Man's garden

Fierce Milly had only lived in our street for a week, but she already paraded round as if she owned it. She knew the names of all the cats and dogs, and they knew her and ran away when they heard her coming. Her voice was so loud that everybody closed their windows when she went out to play, in case she woke up all the babies and the grandads.

She called for me and Billy to come out and play nearly every day. We always knew

it was her because she
played a tune on the
knocker and the doorbell.

'Oh for a bit of peace
and quiet,' said Mum. But
Billy said peace and quiet

was boring once you'd got
used to Fierce Milly being
around.

She knew everyone, went
everywhere and was afraid
of nothing. She even went
into the Old Man's garden. Me and Billy
never went in there. Not even after footballs.
We had never even seen the Old Man, and
his garden was really scary. He never cut his
bushes or his grass and a row of big dark
trees frowned out over the top of his garden
wall. And our mum didn't allow us to go in
other people's gardens, even when they
weren't scary.

Fierce Milly said the garden was so wild and scary because the Old Man was an ogre, and that he could make things vanish, especially children. So it wasn't fair when Fierce Milly captured our Billy just before tea-time and tied him to a tree in the Old Man's garden and left him there.

I went to find my friend Joe. Calling for Joe was a good idea. I knew he'd get Billy back, but I had to go the long way round because Fierce Milly was on the warpath in the front street and I

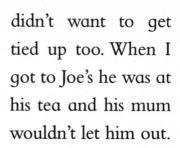

didn't want to get tied up too. When I got to Joe's he was at his tea and his mum wouldn't let him out. So then I thought I would go to the Old Man's garden and shout in to Billy that everything was OK, I was looking for help, it was just hard to find any.

When I got to the Old Man's garden I was really hungry and wanted to go home for tea. I stopped myself thinking of food and climbed on to the wall that is the secret way into the Old Man's garden. There is also a big squeaky iron gate; but you never go into somebody's garden through their gate. That is only for grown-ups and dweebs.

I had never been in the Old Man's garden but I knew the way. You have to wriggle on your tummy along the top of the wall, keeping down flat away from the holly that grows over it, and then there's a place you can jump down. I wasn't going to jump down. I was just going to have an encouraging word with Billy before going home for tea.

But he wasn't there.

I called and called or, rather, whispered and whispered. No Billy. It was true what Fierce Milly had said, then. I couldn't believe it. The Old Man had really vanished our Billy. I jumped down from the wall on to the pavement and ran like the clappers, taking the short way home. I didn't care if fifty Fierce Millys were waving their spears in the street. I was more frightened of the blame I'd get at home for losing our Billy.

And I ran straight into Fierce Milly. I was so cross and hungry and bothered that I just yelled at her, and she jumped out of the way.

'Billy's been vanished,' I said, 'and I'm going to tell. It's all your fault.'

'But no one can open those knots,' Fierce Milly said. 'Those were special elephant-hunters' knots from when my uncle was rescuing elephants in Africa. He showed me

how to make them. I was only trying them out on Billy.'

'Well somebody opened them,' I said.

'Billy might still be in the garden. He might be hiding to frighten you.'

'You know and I know what has happened. The Old Man has vanished him and I'm going to tell.'

'Don't tell,' Fierce Milly said.

'Well sooner or later someone's going to notice he's gone,' I said.

'Come on. We're going to the Old Man's garden. Find a stick.'

I couldn't believe I was going right into the Old Man's garden.

'You first,' Fierce Milly said.

'Will not,' I said. And I meant it, so she didn't argue.

Having Fierce Milly go first made me feel a lot braver and it meant it was her who squashed the slug when she jumped down,

21

and not me.
Nothing sticks
like squashed
slug and she
had it all over
her knee. I
jumped down
behind her
and stayed behind her.

The Old Man's garden is full of big bushes. You can duck down under their branches and get right inside them. They are like brown caves, with the floor made of dry broken leaves. We tiptoed and crawled through all the bushes, me whispering, 'Billy, Billy.' We came to the last bush. It was nearly up against the front window of the Old Man's house.

'Look,' said Milly. 'A clue – on the doorstep. It's my rope with the elephant-hunter's knots.'

Milly's rope lay
along the path, up
the step, and into
the porch.

'He's probably
eaten him by now,' she said, 'and made soup
with his bones.'

I felt like crying but I was too scared. 'My
mum will be raging,' I said.

'Look!' said Fierce Milly, and a strange
thing happened. An old, old hand opened

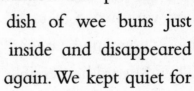

the window and put down a
dish of wee buns just
inside and disappeared
again. We kept quiet for
ages, looking at the wee buns in the dish.

'I'm getting one of those buns,' Fierce
Milly said.

'It's a trap.'

'They might be Billy,' she said.

I hadn't thought of that. If they were Billy

it would be only right to get him back.

Fierce Milly crawled out of the bush. There was an old barrel under the window. She knelt on that and, keeping her head down, reached her arm up, up, up to where the bun dish stood.

'Atchoo!' I sneezed. But when I opened my eyes Fierce Milly had vanished! Oh no, it had happened again. Then I heard her terrible roar, and the barrel

started yelling and kicking, so I knew she had fallen into it. The Old Man would hear all the noise and come running out and catch her. This was no time to be scared. I became Rescue Susan and roared as loud as

24

any elephant knotted in a
rope and leaped out of the
bush to free Fierce Milly.

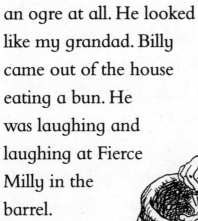

She was the right way
up by then, but all I could see of her was her
face peeping over the edge of the barrel. She
was very cobwebby. She wasn't so fierce
now.

'Get me out of here,' she bawled, and then
her eyes went all round and big and her
mouth made a capital O.

'Indeed I will,' said a big laughing voice.
It was the Old Man and he didn't look like
an ogre at all. He looked
like my grandad. Billy
came out of the house
eating a bun. He
was laughing and
laughing at Fierce
Milly in the
barrel.

Billy said could we keep her in there and just give her a bun now and again? She could be a zoo.

The Old Man hooked her out and stood her on her feet. She still had squashed slug on her knee and cobwebs on her jumper and old leaves in her hair. She looked very sorry for herself.

'Lost your voice, young lady?' asked the Old Man.

'Thank you for getting me out of the barrel,' she said in a tiny, tiny voice.

'A good hose-down and you'll be right as rain,' the Old Man said. 'I wonder who tied poor Billy to a tree? Keep away from dangerous women, young Billy. Now, off home with the lot of you.'

So we went home for tea. Fierce Milly came too. Mum made her wash her hands three times, and her face. She soon looked normal, but her voice stayed tiny all the way through tea.

'Do you think she'll be fierce again tomorrow?' Billy said to me later.

'I hope so,' I said.

3 Fierce Milly and the dinosaur

One day Fierce Milly said that she had a dinosaur in her backyard.

Billy said, 'What sort is it?'

'A diplostegohocuspocusdocus.' She said that Billy and me could go and listen to it walking about in there if we gave her ten pence. We didn't have ten pence and I said I didn't want to listen to some stupid old dinosaur walking about.

'And I bet it's not a real one, anyway,' I said.

28

Fierce Milly huffed and said she was going off to play with the dinosaur on her own. He was more fun.

Then Billy started finding things. He found ten pence on the pavement. 'Now I can go and hear the dinosaur!' he said.

'I bet there is no dinosaur,' I said. 'I bet she's making it up, like the yellow hand, like the Old Man being an ogre. That wasn't real. I bet even her uncle isn't real.'

But Billy wouldn't listen. 'The dinosaur might be real,' he said. 'You don't know it's not real.' And he ran away on up the street after Fierce Milly and gave her the ten

29

pence so that he could go and listen to the maybe-dinosaur.

He had to meet her at the yellow door in the back lane in half an hour. He made me go with him, just in case. The yellow door looked very ordinary, considering there was supposed to be a dinosaur in there. Fierce

Milly was not pleased to see me.

'Only people who believe in the dinosaur are allowed to listen to it,' she said to Billy. 'Your big sister has to go and wait up at the end of the lane.'

'Can it get out?' Billy asked.

'Only if I let it,' she said.

'Won't it eat you?' Billy asked.

'No, silly. It's the sort of dinosaur that only eats turnips and cabbages and dandelion leaves. Like a rabbit, only bigger, only enormous. It's so big you can't see the whole of it all at once. That's why you're only allowed to listen to it.'

'It's OK, then. You wait at the end of the lane,' Billy said to me. 'But don't go away.'

Fierce Milly said that the dinosaur was asleep and that she was going in now to wake it up. Billy went and stood on the far side of the lane, away from the yellow door. I went and waited up at the far end of the lane.

Billy was very still. I knew he would hardly be breathing. Even up at the end of the lane I could hear Fierce Milly's loud voice.

'Come on, dinosaur, wakey, wakey.' That voice would wake a fossil.

And then it happened. We heard it. Clump, clump, clump – big and echoey in Fierce Milly's backyard. Clump, clump, clump. I had never heard such loud feet.

Billy jumped the height of himself and then he turned and ran right past me. I ran after him. He ran all the way home without stopping and I couldn't catch up with him. He ran up the back lane, round the side of the houses, round the corner, up the street,

32

up our garden,
through the door
and straight up the
stairs into bed and
under the blanket.
I got him out from
under the blanket with
some sweeties
because I
wanted to talk
about the
amazing
dinosaur.

'She's really got a dinosaur. Imagine! It's brilliant,' I said.

'I don't like it,' Billy said. 'I don't like that dinosaur. I want it to go away. Supposing it gets out. Supposing it follows us home.'

'Don't be daft,' I said. 'Mum wouldn't allow a dinosaur in the house. Fierce Milly's lucky her mum lets her keep it.'

'Our mum wouldn't allow us a dinosaur in the backyard,' said Billy.

'She wouldn't allow us a dog, or a cat,' I said.

'Or a beetle in a matchbox, or a snail in a jamjar, or a  worm in a bucket, or a germ in a sneeze,' said Billy. He cheered up after that because he likes lists.

The next day Billy found a turnip in the street.

'I'm always finding things,' he said. He was very pleased. The turnip must have

fallen out of someone's
shopping. It was still in its
brown paper bag.

'Let's go and give it to
Fierce Milly's dinosaur,' I
said.

'I don't want to,' said Billy.

'Oh, come on, sure there's nothing else
you can do with a turnip anyway.'

So we went up the back lane with the
turnip. It took a couple of goes to throw it
high enough to fly over the wall. We could
hear it thump down on to the ground and
then roll across the backyard. We flattened
our ears to the yellow
door, waiting for the
clump, clump, clump
and the munch,
munch, munch of the
turnip being eaten.
Nothing.

'Maybe the dinosaur's asleep,' I said. 'Let's climb up and look.'

Fierce Milly's back wall is easy to climb because it's made of old rough stonework and the top of it is very broad. Me and Billy perched up there and looked down into the yard. We couldn't see the whole yard because of the shed roof being in the way. There was no dinosaur, only a few old plastic plant-pots and gardening things, and a broken bicycle, and the turnip lying in a grating.

'The dinosaur must be in the shed,' said Billy.

'Maybe it will wake up and come out to eat the turnip.'

'I don't want to see it,' said Billy.

'Well shut your eyes, then.'

Then we heard Fierce Milly's loud voice. She was up at the far end of the back lane, bringing my other friend Joe to hear the dinosaur. We had plenty of time to lie down flat on the top of the wall where she couldn't see us.

'All I've got is five pence and a sharpener,' Joe said.

'That's OK,' said Fierce Milly. 'You can listen for a short time. But you have to stay out here.'

'Where do you get dinosaurs from, then?' asked Joe.

'I hatched it out of an egg,' said Fierce Milly.

'Where did you get the egg?' asked Joe.

'If you ask any more questions you'll use up your whole five pence and not get to hear the dinosaur.'

'I was only asking,' said Joe.

'I think I hear it waking up now,' said Fierce Milly. 'You wait here.' And she went into the backyard below us. She disappeared behind the shed and we could hear her calling, 'Nice dinosaur, wake up now, time for walkies.'

Billy's eyes were shut so tightly they were nearly inside out.

'I don't want to see it,' he whispered.

'Then don't look,' I whispered back. But I was going to look.

Clump, clump, clump. The dinosaur was

coming out of the shed.
My heart was going thump,
thump, thump, and
my eyes closed
themselves tight all
by themselves. But
I just had to see
this dinosaur.

When I did
open my eyes,
I laughed and
laughed. And Billy's eyes flew open to see
why and then he was laughing too. It was
Fierce Milly making the clumping noise.
She had her feet stuck into two big plastic
flowerpots and was walking around
clumping: clump, clump, clump. Fierce Milly
was the dinosaur. The flowerpots made very
funny shoes, and a very loud noise.

We shouted, 'Dinosaur feet! Dinosaur feet!'
'Get off my wall,' shouted Fierce Milly,

and she came clumping out of the backyard to get us, but she forgot about Joe.

Joe was raging at being tricked, and he made Fierce Milly give back the five pence and the sharpener and Billy's ten pence. Then he started laughing because he suddenly thought it was very funny. And Fierce Milly had a laugh too and we all laughed. We took turns with the flowerpots at clumping about like a dinosaur, until her mum said that that was enough of that awful noise and told us to go away.

On our way home, Billy stopped at the long grass at the far end of the back lane.

'Look,' he said. 'I've found something again. It's a big speckledy egg in the grass. What sort of egg do you think it is?'

'Will you stop finding things,' I said.

'Leave it alone. It might belong to someone.'

'Or something,' Billy said.

The next day we called for Fierce Milly to walk to school with her, but we all went to look at the big egg on the way.

It was gone.

Billy said, 'Do you think it has hatched?'

Fierce Milly said, 'Yes, that's very possible. And after school I'm going to catch whatever it is and put it in my backyard, and you two can help me look after it. My uncle that came back from Africa showed me how to hunt wild animals.'

I wish her uncle would go back to Africa, even if he's not real.

4 Fierce Milly and the magic wings

At school Fierce Milly wriggled and talked and dropped her pencil all the time. Miss said she was impossible and made her sit beside me because I was sensible and would be a good influence. This did not work. Then one day Miss said that our class was going to be in the school play and that only those who were good and quiet would be in it. That worked. Fierce Milly really, really wanted to be in the play.

Miss held a meeting at break-time for anyone who wanted a part. Me and Fierce Milly went. Fierce Milly put her hand up first. 'Miss, Miss, my uncle from Africa can do a special effect for the play.'

'Not now, Mildred,' said Miss, and we all laughed because when Miss calls Fierce Milly Mildred, it always makes her go quiet. But when we call her Mildred, she roars.

Miss said that Fierce Milly had to be the mushroom in the play and all the rest of us would be fairies and that our mums had to get us white sticky-out frocks with fairy wings on.

Fierce Milly said she didn't want to be a mushroom. Mushrooms were boring. Miss said she had to be the mushroom because she was the only one that fitted the mushroom costume from last year, and the mushroom was the most important vegetable on stage, and all the fairies had to dance round it. So Fierce Milly said that was all right then, fairies were boring, and what about her uncle's special effect?

'Not now, Mildred,' said Miss.

I wish Fierce Milly would shut up about her uncle. He's too strange to be true. Nobody's uncle could do all those things. She says he learned from a witch doctor how to read minds. And he hatched an ostrich egg in his pocket and, when the ostrich grew up, he taught it to speak. I think he's just not possible.

We had to have our costumes ready

for the dress rehearsal. My mum
got me a white sticky-out frock
and made me a great pair of
fairy wings with cellophane and
wire coat hangers bent into wing
shapes. She stuck shiny silver stars
all over the wings and sewed
them to the back of the frock. She
hung it on the hook on my
bedroom door and I couldn't get
to sleep for ages because I kept
looking at it. The wings twinkled
in the dark. I thought they might

be magic.

I told everyone at school about the great wings my mum made and Fierce Milly said she was coming to my house to have a look at them. I didn't want her to come because she would only say that they were boring. But being not wanted never stopped Fierce Milly, so she came to look. She said they were OK and they did have a sort of magic look about them and could she try them on? I wouldn't let her.

I was really excited when the time came for the dress rehearsal. I wanted to try the frock on at home first to see myself in the mirror, and just as Mum pulled up the zip – zap! It broke.

'It's just as well it happened now and not

on stage,' Mum said. 'I can sew you into it and you can wear it down to school. Sure it's only round the corner.'

'But everybody will be looking at me,' I said.

'Of course they will, it's a lovely frock. Now off you go,' Mum said.

I couldn't do it. I couldn't walk down the front street with fairy wings on. All the magic went out of the wings. It was different from being in the play where everyone else had wings too.

What if Fierce Milly saw me? She'd be staring and pointing. What if Cecil Nutt and his gang saw me? Cecil Nutt's gang was only Joe, who was sometimes my friend if Cecil Nutt wasn't around. But they'd pass smart remarks about my wings and that would make me go all red.

★ ★ ★

My luck was out. There at the end of the street, sitting on the windowsill of the corner shop, just waiting to see what they could see, were Cecil Nutt and Joe. I could feel my wings growing bigger and bigger and me growing smaller and smaller, until I was nothing but a big pair of fairy wings walking up the street.

Then I heard feet coming up behind me. It was Fierce Milly. She was going to pass smart remarks, too. But she said, 'Never you mind those two looking at your wings. Just stick

your nose in the air and walk past swanky. Like me.' Then she linked her arm through mine and hooshed me on up the street, the both of us walking swanky, right past the corner shop, right past the noses of Cecil Nutt and his gang. Sometimes Fierce Milly was almost my best friend.

But she spoiled it. Just as we walked past she announced, 'And you needn't be pass-remarkable about her wings. They're for real.'

'Go on,' said Cecil Nutt.

'They are so too,' said Fierce Milly. 'She can fly.'

They stood still, gobsmacked, looking after us as we went on down the hill to school.

'Why did you say that?' I asked.

'Well, your wings look as good as real,' she said.

'Sure you know I can't fly.'

'*They* don't.'

'Well they soon enough will. Going about saying I can fly when I can't. Look at the trouble you've got me in. Stop making things up. You're not my friend any more.' And I stomped on ahead of her into school.

The rehearsal did not go well for me. I kept dancing the wrong way round the mushroom because all I could think of was Cecil Nutt and Joe waiting outside to see me fly home. Miss made me sit out because all the other fairies kept tripping over me.

'Excellent mushroom, Mildred,' Miss said at the end of the practice. 'That's the first time you've done anything right in school.'

Fierce Milly smirked.

'But what will I do with you?' she said to me. 'You've suddenly grown two left feet. I don't think that you can be a dancing fairy tomorrow.'

'Miss, Miss, I know what she can do!' Fierce Milly said.

'Not now, Mildred, I'm thinking.'

'Miss, Miss. The special effect! Wait till you hear!' And Fierce Milly rushed up to her and whispered something in Miss's ear, and Miss's eyes got all round and pleased.

'Why, Mildred! That would be wonderful! I must make the arrangements right away. You two come early tomorrow, and bring your uncle.'

'Bring your uncle! Bring your uncle! But he's not real,' I said after the rehearsal. Then Fierce Milly whispered the secret to me as well.

'Oh, I hope that's true, I really, really hope that's true,' I said.

Cecil Nutt and Joe were still waiting outside the school. 'Waiting to see you fly home,' Fierce Milly whispered to me. And then she shouted out to Cecil Nutt's gang, 'Go away! She only flies when she wants to. Maybe she'll fly tomorrow night at the school play, and maybe she'll not.' She winked at me and I winked back. She was

nearly my best friend
again.

Fierce Milly's uncle from Africa
was really real. He was waiting
for us at school the next day, to
practise the special effect.
Then it was time to get
ready for the play. We all
got our costumes on and took turns peeping
out through the gap in the curtains to see
the people coming in. Mum and our Billy
were there and Fierce Milly's mum was
there and right in the very front row, leaning
back in their chairs with their feet up on our
stage, were Cecil Nutt and Joe.

It was time for the play to start and I had
to go backstage and wait with Fierce Milly's
uncle for the special effect.

Then it happened. I flew. Cecil Nutt and
Joe had a serious case of popped out eyes

53

and open mouths as I flew
right over the dancing
fairies and the mushroom.
I waved at them. I waved
at my mum and our Billy.
I waved at everybody
and the mushroom fell
over trying to see me from
under her big mushroom
hat and all the fairies and
Miss had to pick her up,
and I flew back in
and Milly's uncle
landed me safely
behind the scenery.

It wasn't magic,
though it was
as good as
magic.

I had a special harness under my white
sticky-out frock and there was a hook at the
back for fixing to a
thin strong wire

that went up to the ceiling. Milly's uncle held the other end of the wire and, when he pulled, I flew. He said he had learned to do that when he was once in a circus.

'Was the circus in Africa?' I asked Fierce Milly.

'Oh, I don't know,' she said. 'Sometimes he makes things up.'

Fierce Milly is my very best friend in the world now, and I'm going to let her wear the magic fairy wings whenever she wants.